THUDD

Hiya! My name Thudd. Best robot friend of Drewd. Thudd know lots of stuff. How stars get born. Where planets come from. What happened to dinosaurs.

Drewd and Unkie Al like to invent stuff. Unkie invent time machine. Oop! Drewd have snack accident. Drewd and Oody go back in time! Want to come? Turn page, please!

Get lost with
Andrew, Judy, and Thudd
in all their exciting adventures!

Andrew Lost on the Dog
Andrew Lost in the Bathroom
Andrew Lost in the Kitchen
Andrew Lost in the Garden
Andrew Lost Under Water
Andrew Lost in the Whale
Andrew Lost on the Reef
Andrew Lost in the Deep
Andrew Lost in Time
Andrew Lost on Earth
Andrew Lost with the Dinosaurs

AND COMING SOON!
Andrew Lost in the Ice Age

ANDREW LOST

11

WITH THE DINOSAURS

BY J. C. GREENBURG

ILLUSTRATED
BY JAN GERARDI

A STEPPING STONE BOOK™

Random House New York

To Dan, Zack, and the real Andrew,
with a galaxy of love.
To the children who read these books: I wish
you wonderful questions. Questions are
telescopes into the universe!
—J.C.G.

To Cathy Goldsmith, with many thanks.
—J.G.

Text copyright © 2005 by J. C. Greenburg.
Illustrations copyright © 2005 by Jan Gerardi.
All rights reserved under International and Pan-American Copyright
Conventions. Published in the United States by Random House
Children's Books, a division of Random House, Inc., New York, and
simultaneously in Canada by Random House of Canada Limited,
Toronto.

www.randomhouse.com/kids/AndrewLost
www.AndrewLost.com

Library of Congress Cataloging-in-Publication Data
Greenburg, J. C. (Judith C.)
With the dinosaurs / by J. C. Greenburg ; illustrated by
Jan Gerardi. — 1st ed.
   p.   cm. — (Andrew Lost ; 11)   A Stepping Stone book.
SUMMARY: When Beeper accidentally releases the escape hatch to
the Time-A-Tron, the time travelers must protect themselves from
the world's most fearsome creature, Tyrannosaurus rex.
ISBN 0-375-82951-2 (trade) — ISBN 0-375-92951-7 (lib. bdg.)
[1. Tyrannosaurus rex—Fiction. 2. Dinosaurs—Fiction.
3. Time travel—Fiction. 4. Cousins—Fiction.] I. Gerardi, Jan, ill.
II. Title. III. Series: Greenburg, J. C. (Judith C.). Andrew Lost ; v 11.
PZ7.G82785Wi 2005   [Fic]—dc22   2004024350

Printed in the United States of America
First Edition   10 9 8 7 6 5 4 3

RANDOM HOUSE and colophon are registered trademarks and A STEPPING
STONE BOOK and colophon are trademarks of Random House, Inc.
ANDREW LOST is a trademark of J. C. Greenburg.

CONTENTS

ANDREW'S WORLD

Andrew Dubble

Andrew is ten years old, but he's been inventing things since he was four. Andrew's inventions usually get him into trouble, like the time he shrunk himself, his cousin Judy, and his little silver robot Thudd smaller than a beetle's brain.

Today a problem with a snack has sent Andrew traveling through time. He's landed 65 million years ago—the age of dinosaurs!

Judy Dubble

Judy is Andrew's thirteen-year-old cousin. At nine o'clock, she got into her pajamas in a cabin in Montana.

A few hours later, she was staring into the eyes of a humongous Alamosaurus. According to Judy, it's all Andrew's fault.

Thudd

The Handy Ultra-Digital Detective. Thudd is a super-smart robot and Andrew's best friend. He has helped to save Andrew and Judy from deadly octopuses, killer jellyfish, and the giant squid. But can he save them from being eaten by a Tyrannosaurus?

Uncle Al

Andrew and Judy's uncle is a top-secret scientist. He invented Thudd and the Time-A-Tron time-travel machine. But before he finished the Time-A-Tron, he was kidnapped and hidden in one of Earth's ice ages! Will Andrew and Judy be able to find him?

The Time-A-Tron

It looks like a giant cooking timer, but it's really a time-travel machine. Too bad Uncle Al got kidnapped before he could make sure it worked!

Doctor Kron-Tox

The mysterious Doctor Kron-Tox invented a time machine, too—the Tick-Tox Box. He's used it to kidnap Uncle Al and his partner, Winka Wilde. But why?

Beeper Jones

Andrew and Judy found nine-year-old Beeper 360 million years ago. He likes to collect dog-sized scorpions and six-foot centipedes, and—oh yes—he's Doctor Kron-Tox's nephew. Other than that, he's not a bad kid.

1

THIS IS *BIG*!

"Wowzers schnauzers!" shouted ten-year-old Andrew Dubble. Huge eyes were staring at him through the dome of the Time-A-Tron time-travel vehicle. "I think it's a brontosaur!"

The Time-A-Tron had landed in a forest 65 million years ago. It had also landed on the long, thick, scaly tail of a humongous dinosaur!

The dark reptile eyes staring in at Andrew did not look pleased.

Judy, Andrew's thirteen-year-old cousin, leaned forward in her seat. "Cheese Louise!" she said. "Its neck is as long as a bus!"

"That's no brontosaur," said Beeper Jones. Beeper was a nine-year-old boy they had rescued 300 million years ago.

Beeper pointed a gadget that looked like a remote control at the long-necked creature.

ping . . . ping . . . ping . . .

"The DNA Detector says it's an Alamosaurus," said Beeper.

meep . . . "Alamosaurus look like brontosaur," squeaked a voice from Andrew's pocket. It was Thudd, Andrew's little silver robot and best friend. "Long as two school buses. Weigh as much as forty cars."

AL-uh-moe-SAW-rus

Thudd pointed to a picture of an Alamosaurus on his face screen.

bong . . . "Brontosaurs are not alive now," said the echoey voice of the Time-A-Tron. "They have been extinct for eighty million years."

The Alamosaurus opened its mouth. Inside were short, stumpy teeth.

"It looks angry enough to eat us," said Judy.

meep . . . "Alamosaurus is plant-eater," said Thudd. "Use teeth to grab leaves, not chew. Got stones inside stomach to grind up food."

Suddenly the Alamosaurus smacked its tail on the ground. The Time-A-Tron flipped into the air like a pancake!

The Time-A-Tron came down on its side, whammed into a tree, and rolled downhill.

"Yerggghhh!" yelled Andrew.

"Burf!" said Judy.

"Whoopee!" yelled Beeper from the backseat. "This is more fun than a roller coaster. It's our own dino coaster!"

Andrew smiled.

The Time-A-Tron slammed into a small hill.

Andrew, Judy, and Beeper stayed in their seats until they stopped feeling dizzy. Then Andrew unbuckled his seat belt.

"We'd better get out and start looking for Professor Wilde," he said.

Earlier, the DNA Detector had detected a human. There weren't supposed to be any humans on Earth now. But Professor Winka Wilde had been kidnapped by Beeper's uncle, the evil Doctor Kron-Tox, and hidden in time. If there was a human here, it had to be her.

bong . . . "Wait, children!" said the Time-A-Tron. "I cannot allow you to leave. It is dangerous out there. You could be trampled by an Alamosaurus."

"Naaaah," said Beeper. "Those big old plant-eaters are pretty slow."

"Yeah," said Andrew. "We can see it coming and get out of the way."

bong . . . "I do not want to frighten you," said the Time-A-Tron, "but we have arrived at the time of the most fearsome creature that has ever lived—the Tyrannosaurus rex."

meep . . . "Name mean 'tyrant lizard king,'" said Thudd. "Long as railroad car! High as two-story house! Teeth long as bananas! Eat five hundred pounds of meat in one bite!"

tie-RAN-uh-SAW-rus

"Eeeuw!" Judy shivered. "It could eat six Andrews in one chomp."

"I'll check for Tyrannosauruses," said Beeper. He typed "Tyrannosaurus" into the DNA Detector and pressed a button.

ping . . . ping . . . ping . . .

"Hot doggies!" said Beeper. "The DNA Detector says there *is* a Tyrannosaurus out there—and it's real close!"

"How close?" asked Judy.

"Only six feet away!" said Beeper.

Judy rolled her eyes. "If a Tyrannosaurus was six feet away, I think we'd notice," she said.

"Let me see the DNA Detector," said Andrew.

Beeper handed the gadget to Andrew.

Andrew pushed a black button labeled "Find It." A little display blinked "6 Feet."

Andrew looked around. "Maybe this thing doesn't work on Tyrannosauruses," he

said. "Maybe there really aren't any Tyrannosauruses out there. So let's go."

bong . . . "No," said the Time-A-Tron. "I
do not want to explain to Professor Dubble
that his favorite children were eaten by
dinosaurs."

Professor Dubble was Andrew and Judy's
uncle. They called him Uncle Al. Doctor
Kron-Tox had snatched him, too, and hidden
him in an ice age.

"But we've got to rescue Winka Wilde,"
pleaded Andrew. "Uncle Al wouldn't like it if
we left his partner stuck here."

bong . . . "Professor Wilde is a brilliant scientist," said the Time-A-Tron. "If she is here,
she will find us."

"I wanna take a picture of that Alamosaurus," said Beeper. "If my camera still
works."

bong . . . "Absolutely not!" said the Time-
A-Tron.

Beeper sighed. "Okay," he said. "I guess you're right. Where's the bathroom? I gotta go."

bong . . . "It is in the bottom compartment, Master Beeper," said the Time-A-Tron. "Behind the bulge labeled 'Tachyons.'"

Beeper pulled up the door in the floor and went below.

BZERK! BZERK! BZERK!

An alarm was going off!

bong . . . "Noooo!" cried the Time-A-Tron. "Master Beeper has activated the emergency escape!"

2 LOOKING FOR TROUBLE

Andrew and Judy peered into the bottom compartment. The oval door to the outside was open.

"Beeper!" yelled Andrew.

"Come back, you little bozo!" yelled Judy.

There was no answer. They looked out through the clear dome of the Time-A-Tron.

Andrew spied a spot of orange moving through the tall ferns. It was Beeper's T-shirt.

"I see the little creep!" said Judy.

"Now there are *two* people we have to look for," said Andrew. "We've got to go."

bong . . . "Children!" said the Time-A-

Tron. "In this forest live the fiercest meat-eaters on Earth. You have nothing to protect you. Your colorful pajamas are signs that say 'Here I am! Eat me!'"

"It's not our fault that we're wearing our stupid pajamas," said Judy. "We were getting ready for bed when Doctor Kron-Tox dragged off Uncle Al."

Andrew looked out through the Time-A-Tron's dome.

"There are lots of big plants out there," he said. "We'll creep around under the tall ferns. If there are any Tyrannosauruses, they won't see us."

meep . . . "Tyrannosaurus got big sense of smell," said Thudd. "Use smell to hunt."

"Mmmmmm . . . ," hummed the Time-A-Tron. "There *may* be a way for you to be safe out there."

"What is it?" asked Andrew.

bong . . . "First," said the Time-A-Tron, "you must promise to do exactly as I say."

Judy folded her arms across her chest. "I don't promise anything before I know what it is," she said.

bong . . . "You are wise, Miss Judy," said the Time-A-Tron. "But I must have your promise."

"It's okay," said Andrew to Judy. "The Time-A-Tron wouldn't tell us to do anything stupid."

"Oh, all right," said Judy.

bong . . . "This will not be pleasant," said the Time-A-Tron. "But it could keep you alive. Listen closely.

"As we were rolling along the ground, we ran over a pile of Alamosaurus . . . um . . . dung."

"You mean poop?" asked Andrew.

bong . . . "Yes," said the Time-A-Tron. "I must insist that you cover yourselves with Alamosaurus poop before you go into the forest."

"*Whaaaat?*" yelled Judy.

"Woofers!" said Andrew.

bong . . . "Most animals will stay away from, er, poop. It will be like a smelly suit of armor."

"No *way*!" said Judy.

Andrew looked at Judy. "You promised," he said. "Maybe we can, uh, hold our noses."

Judy thought for a second. "How about this?" she said. "We can disguise ourselves as ferns. We'll stick giant fern fronds into the waistbands of our pajamas."

bong . . . "Not good enough, Miss Judy. The Tyrannosaurus and other dinosaurs will still sniff you out."

"Well," she said, "how about if we dip the ferns in the dino poop."

bong . . . "Good thinking, Miss Judy!" said the Time-A-Tron. "You are very brave. Be careful."

"We will," said Andrew. "Now where's that dino poop?"

bong . . . "It is back there," said the Time-A-Tron.

A silver tube poked up from the control panel. Out of the silver tube shot a thin ray of green light. It zoomed through the Time-A-Tron's dome and into the forest.

"We'll find it," said Andrew. He slipped through the door in the floor.

bong . . . "Just follow your noses," said the Time-A-Tron.

Judy opened a small door under the control panel. A pair of beady black eyes stared up at her. A pointy brown nose twitched. It was the shrew that had gotten into the Time-A-Tron when it was still in Uncle Al's laboratory.

"You stay right here till we get back," said Judy. She closed the little door, then followed Andrew into the lower compartment.

Andrew was poking around. "Um, I don't see the owl," he said.

A little owl had followed the shrew into the Time-A-Tron before they left Montana.

"I'll bet it got out when Beeper left," said Judy.

bong . . . "Very bad news, Master Andrew," said the Time-A-Tron. "There are no owls on Earth sixty-five million years ago. At this time, the ancestors of humans are creeping around in the forests. Your little owl may eat them! Because of this tiny owl, it is possible that *you* may not exist!"

"Uh-oh," said Andrew. "That's pretty weird. We'd better find that owl."

bong . . . "Good luck, little Dubbles," said the Time-A-Tron. "Much depends on you."

Andrew and Judy stepped through the oval door to the outside.

bong . . . The door closed behind them.

The sun was baking hot and the air was sticky. The ground was damp and swampy.

Andrew sniffed a spicy smell.

"Pines!" said Andrew, looking up at the tall trees.

"OUCH!" yelled Judy, slapping her neck. "I just got bitten by a monster mosquito!"

meep . . . "Lotsa new stuff since we get stuck three hundred million years ago," said Thudd. "Got pine trees and maple trees and oak trees. Got flowers now. Got lots more insects, too. Got mosquitoes that bite through dinosaur skin!"

crick . . . crick . . . crick . . .

Sounds were coming from the hill that the Time-A-Tron had rolled into. It was actually a pile of leaves and moss. Andrew went up to take a closer look.

crick . . . crick . . . crick . . .

A chunk of moss slid away. There was something smooth and white beneath it.

"Wowzers schnauzers!" said Andrew. "It's an egg! A huge egg!"

3 EGGS-ACTLY RIGHT!

The egg trembled. A crack zigzagged across its top.

"It's hatching!" said Judy.

crick . . . crack . . . crack . . .

Now there was a hole in the top of the egg. From the hole poked a head as big as a puppy's. But this head was scaly. Sharp little teeth hung down from the top of its mouth.

Its bright black eyes looked up at Judy and blinked. It gripped the edge of the shell with the two teeny fingers at the ends of its tiny little arms.

Judy slapped her hand over her mouth. "It's a . . ."

meep . . . "Tyrannosaurus baby," said
Thudd.

"Beeper was right!" said Andrew. "*This* is
what the DNA Detector was picking up!"

meep . . . "Dinosaur baby called chick,"
said Thudd. "Just like bird. Dinosaurs are
great-great-great-great-great-grandparents of
birds. When you see bird, you see little
dinosaur!"

crick . . . *crick* . . .

The shell cracked apart and the tiny dinosaur took a few wobbly steps toward Judy.

Judy backed away. "It's not even as high

as my knee and it wants to eat me!" she said.

meep . . . "Maybe not want to eat you," said Thudd. "Maybe chick think Oody is Tyrannosaurus mom."

Judy frowned. "Are you saying I look like a Tyrannosaurus?" she asked.

"Noop! Noop! Noop!" said Thudd. "When bird chick hatch out of egg, chick think first thing it see is mom. If baby duck see human first, baby duck think human is mom."

As Judy stepped back, the Tyrannosaurus chick followed.

Suddenly it lurched at Judy, opened its mouth, and bit the leg of her pajamas with its sharp little teeth.

"NO!" said Judy loudly. She tapped the Tyrannosaurus on its snout.

Unnk! it grunted as it shredded Judy's pajama leg.

"He doesn't think I'm Mom," said Judy.

"He thinks I'm lunch."

Just then, a yellow butterfly fluttered between Judy and the Tyrannosaurus. The baby dinosaur pawed the air trying to grab it. The butterfly darted off and the Tyrannosaurus followed it.

Judy turned to Andrew. "You know, its mother could be back any minute to feed it."

meep . . . "Nobody know if Tyrannosaurus

mom take care of Tyrannosaurus babies," said Thudd.

"Well," said Andrew, "if there's a little one here, there are big ones around somewhere. We'd better find that dino poop."

Andrew and Judy followed the Time-A-Tron's bright green beam up a hill.

"Wait a minute," said Judy, stopping under a fern that towered over her head. She snapped off a bunch of fronds and handed half of them to Andrew.

It wasn't long before the beam—and their noses—led them to a huge pile of brown stuff.

"Eeeeuuw!" said Judy.

"Yuckers!" said Andrew.

meep . . . "Gotta do it!" said Thudd.

Andrew and Judy looked at each other. Then Andrew swished his fern fronds across the poop. Judy did the same. They stuck the ends of the fronds into the waistbands of their pajamas.

Judy pinched her nose with her fingers.

Andrew typed "Beeper Jones" into the DNA Detector and pressed the Find It button. He moved the detector slowly in a circle.

ping . . . ping . . . ping . . .

"6,000 Feet" blinked on the display.

"Wowzers!" said Andrew. "Beeper's more than a mile away!"

Andrew's and Judy's slippers were slippery, but they started slogging their way in the direction of the signal.

Judy shook her head. "The ferns and bushes are so tall and thick we can't even tell where we're going."

"I see a path," said Andrew.

He pushed his way to a place where the ferns were squashed flat.

"Uh-oh," said Andrew.

In the middle of the flattened plants were gigantic holes—footprints! The three-toed footprints of something enormous!

4 ON SHAKY GROUND

meep . . . "Tyrannosaurus footprints!" said Thudd.

Andrew leaned down to take a closer look.

"Wowzers schnauzers!" he hollered. "There are sneaker prints inside this gigunda footprint! This has to be the way that Beeper went."

Judy shook her head.

"I can't believe we've gone back to the beginning of the universe in our pajamas, we almost got bitten by a six-foot centipede, and now we're disguised as poopy ferns following

the footsteps of a Tyrannosaurus. This is *so* your fault, Bug-Brain."

Andrew shrugged. "We have to rescue Professor Wilde and Uncle Al," he said.

"Cheese Louise!" said Judy, looking down. "We can *both* fit inside the Tyrannosaurus footprint!"

"Yeah," said Andrew. "Beeper would fit, too."

Suddenly the big purple button in the middle of Thudd's chest popped open and a purple beam zoomed out. A smiling Uncle Al was at the end of it.

"Hey there!" he said.

The last time Andrew and Judy had seen him, Uncle Al had been completely wrapped in a furry skin to keep warm. Icicles had been hanging off his nose. Now there were no icicles and the furry skin was tossed over his shoulders.

"Hi, Uncle Al!" said Andrew.

"Hiya, Unkie!" said Thudd.

"Wait till you hear where we're stuck now!" said Judy.

Uncle Al's eyebrows came together in one fuzzy line. "Where *are* you?" he asked.

Uncle Al was using his Hologram Helper to communicate with Andrew and Judy. He could hear them, but he couldn't see them.

"We're walking in the footsteps of a Tyrannosaurus rex!" said Judy.

"We stopped at sixty-five million years ago," said Andrew. "Three hundred million years ago, we picked up Doctor Kron-Tox's nephew, Beeper Jones. He's got a DNA Detector. It gave us a signal that Professor Winka Wilde might be here."

Uncle Al's eyebrows went up. "Professor Wilde!" he exclaimed. "I was going to tell you where she was last time, but my batteries went out."

"And now we have to get Beeper back,

too," Judy said. "The little bozo took off into the forest."

"I know Beeper," said Uncle Al. "He visited my lab when he was knee-high. An . . . um . . . interesting boy. He was nutty about dinosaurs. He found a fossil dinosaur egg when he was only three years old."

"Wowzers!" said Andrew.

"He's still an annoying little creep," said Judy. "But I guess we can't let him get eaten by a Tyrannosaurus."

Uncle Al shook his head. "You kids are amazing," said Uncle Al. "But I'm very worried."

"Oh, we've got protection," said Judy, rolling her eyes. "We're wearing fern fronds dipped in Alamosaurus poop. The ferns were my idea. The Time-A-Tron came up with the poop idea."

Uncle Al smiled. "Judy, you're a brilliant young woman," he said. "And the Time-A-

Tron is very intelligent. But the most important thing is that it cares.

"By the way, Doctor Kron-Tox stole a DNA Detector from my laboratory. He must have given it to Beeper.

"But that's good. The DNA Detector has the records of our family DNA and Winka Wilde's, too. I'm sure Doctor Kron-Tox added Beeper's DNA and maybe his own. So you'll be able to find . . ."

The Uncle Al hologram was getting fuzzy. Uncle Al's voice sounded far away.

"Uncle Al!" shouted Judy. "Don't go!"

The last words they heard were ". . . batteries not . . ."

The Uncle Al hologram disappeared into a purple fog.

Swsssshhhh . . .

The sound was coming from the bushes.

Akkkkk! Akkkkk! Akkkkk!

Screeee! Screeee!

A possum-like creature ran by them. Something was chasing after it! It looked like a bird and was about the size of a big chicken. But this animal had few feathers and arms with claws at the end!

meep . . . "Bambiraptor dinosaur chase mammal called Alphadon," said Thudd. "Mammals very small in dinosaur time."

BAM-bee-RAP-tur

AL-fuh-dahn

"Is the little Alphadon one of our ances-tors?" asked Andrew.

"Noop!" said Thudd. "Drewd and Oody ancestor is little animal that look like shrew."

Andrew pressed the DNA Detector's Find It button again to get Beeper's location.

ping . . . ping . . . ping . . .

Following the signal, Andrew left the path and pushed his way through the ferns to a patch of sand.

Suddenly the ground beneath his feet felt as squishy as a bowl of pudding.

"Yikes!" yelled Andrew.

The sand was slurping him down!

THUMMMPP . . .
THUMMMPP . . .
THUMMMPP . . .

"Andrew!" yelled Judy. "Get out of there!"

"I can't!" said Andrew.

meep . . . "Quicksand!" said Thudd.

Andrew kicked his feet to keep from sinking, but the harder he kicked, the quicker he sank.

Andrew tossed the DNA Detector to Judy. Then he pulled Thudd out of his pocket and put him on top of his head to keep him dry. Thudd was never supposed to get wet.

meep . . . "Drewd can float on top of quicksand," said Thudd. "Quicksand is plain sand with lotsa water underneath. Drewd gotta stop kicking. Kicking make Drewd get sucked down fast, fast, fast! Drewd gotta move slow, slow, slow. Then float."

Andrew stopped kicking. As soon as he did, he stopped sinking. He put his head back. Thudd crept onto his forehead. Andrew slowly pulled his legs up.

"YES!" said Andrew. He floated on his back and pushed the sand with his hands. Soon he arrived at the edge of the small pool of quicksand.

Judy leaned toward Andrew. "Grab my hand, Bug-Brain," she said.

Andrew reached out, but he wasn't close enough.

THUMMMPP . . . THUMMMPP . . . THUMMMPP . . .

The ground was shaking.

meep . . . "Is a—"

"Tyrannosaurus rex!" yelled a familiar voice.

It was Beeper! He pushed his way through a clump of ferns toward Judy.

"Pee-yoooo!" he said. "Something smells like dinosaur poop. Hey! It's you!"

"Cheese Louise!" yelled Judy. "Help me drag Bug-Brain out of the quicksand before we all get eaten!"

THUMMMPP . . . THUMMMPP . . . THUMMMPP . . .

The footsteps were faster now. The quicksand jiggled with every step.

RRROHHHURROHRR!

High above the ferns appeared a head as big as a refrigerator. Dark, ragged stuff was stuck between its dagger teeth.

The dinosaur's tiny arms waved excitedly. With each step, it crossed the distance of a room.

Beeper belly-flopped onto the quicksand. Judy was as frozen as a snowman.

"Oody!" shouted Thudd. "Jump in!"

RRROHHHURROHRR!

The sound hurt Andrew's ears. "Judy!" he yelled. "Get in here!"

Judy shivered, dropped the DNA Detector, and plopped into the squishy stuff.

The Tyrannosaurus was at the edge of the quicksand pond. It stopped and looked down.

Andrew heard Judy's teeth chattering. He felt a scream creeping up his throat, but he knew that screaming would be a bad idea.

The huge head lurched toward the sand.

"Hold your breath and duck your head under the quicksand," he whispered to the others.

Andrew took a gulp of air and dunked his head into the cool sand. He tried not to sink too low. He couldn't let himself get sucked into the sand, and he couldn't let Thudd get wet.

RRRRROOOOHHRRR!

The Tyrannosaurus's roar was a rumble in Andrew's mud-filled ears.

Suddenly he felt something scratch his scalp. Could it be . . . *a Tyrannosaurus claw?* In a second, it was gone. And something else was gone—Thudd!

QUICK THINKING

Andrew lifted his head out of the quicksand. He was nose to toes—huge, clawed toes—with the Tyrannosaurus! He looked up past the enormous scaly legs. The dinosaur was holding something shiny in its little front claws.

Thudd! thought Andrew.

The Tyrannosaurus turned and trudged away.

In a few seconds, Judy and Beeper popped to the surface for air. Judy wiped mud from her face. Beeper blew sand out of his nose.

"The Tyrannosaurus has Thudd," Andrew whispered.

Andrew, Judy, and Beeper grabbed branches hanging over the edge of the quicksand and pulled themselves onto solid ground.

"Uh-oh," said Andrew, looking at his bare feet. "The quicksand sucked off my slippers."

"Me too," said Judy. "This is just great. We're barefoot *and* we've lost our poopy ferns."

"I've got an idea how we can get Thudd back," said Andrew. "Run to the other side of the quicksand. Hurry!"

As soon as they reached the far side, Andrew cupped his hands around his mouth and started yelling. "Come and get it, Tyranno-saurus!"

"WHAT?" yelled Judy, clapping her hands over Andrew's mouth.

Andrew pulled her hands away.

"We've got to get the Tyrannosaurus to come back," he said. "When it tries to get us, it'll fall into the quicksand. Then it'll have to use its claws to get out, so it'll have to drop Thudd."

"You've got a major case of nuts-o!" groaned Judy.

"*Super* idea!" said Beeper. "Hooeeey!" he yelled at the top of his lungs. "Hooeeey!"

"Hey, Tyrannosaurus!" yelled Andrew. "Delicious kids here! Here, dino, dino, dino!"

"Oh well," said Judy, rolling her eyes. "Hey, *fatso*!" she yelled. "Get your big, ugly tail over here!"

The Tyrannosaurus stopped. It turned.

RRROHHHURROHRR! it bellowed.

The front of its body leaned forward. Its tail stuck out straight behind. It began racing toward them at an awful speed.

Andrew was sweating with fear, but he waved his hands so the Tyrannosaurus would be sure to see him.

As the Tyrannosaurus lunged toward

them, one of its legs sank into the quicksand! The enormous creature teetered, twisted, and fell onto its back. It was so huge that its body stretched clear across the quicksand pond. The top half crashed to the ground right in front of Andrew.

"Run!" yelled Andrew to Judy and Beeper. "Head for the forest!"

RRROHHHURROHRR!

Andrew was so close that he got a stinky blast of Tyrannosaurus breath. It smelled like a garbage dump.

The dinosaur's little arms were thrashing. It was still holding Thudd in its claws!

Andrew stayed out of range of the sharp hooks. But as they came by, Andrew swatted at Thudd.

Thudd fell to the ground.

meep . . . "Scared! Scared! Scared!" said Thudd.

"It's okay, Thudd," said Andrew, scooping Thudd up.

He ran to the other side of the quicksand pond, picked up the DNA Detector where Judy had dropped it, and raced to catch up with the others.

meep . . . "Hurry, Drewd!" yelped Thudd.

"Tyrannosaurus get out soon!"

"It's going to be one angry dinosaur when it does," said Andrew, running fast.

He was almost out of breath when he heard a voice.

"Hot doggies!" came a shout. It was Beeper.

The ground got swampier as Andrew followed the voice into the forest. He sloshed through the muck in his bare feet.

When he found Beeper and Judy, they were waist-deep in a stream. Judy was washing quicksand out of her hair.

"Come on in!" said Beeper, slapping the water at Andrew.

Andrew looked around. The trees were thick. It didn't look like the Tyrannosaurus could follow them here.

Hmmmmm . . . , thought Andrew. *It sure would feel good to get this quicksand off of me.*

SLUUUUURRRSHHHHHH . . .

Andrew turned toward the slithery sound. Something as big as a giant tree trunk was sliding into the water—a tree trunk with dead-looking eyes. . . .

WHAT A CROC!

EEEK! "Crocodile!" squeaked Thudd. "Super-crocodile! Eat dinosaurs for lunch!"

Andrew had seen crocodiles at the zoo, but this one was so much bigger than those. This crocodile was longer than a dump truck!

Judy didn't see the crocodile. She was digging sand out of her ears.

"Everybody out!" yelled Andrew.

"Eeeeeyah!" yelled Judy as she stumbled and flopped through the water.

Beeper had already sloshed his way to the muddy stream bank.

meep . . . "Crocodile bite strong, strong,

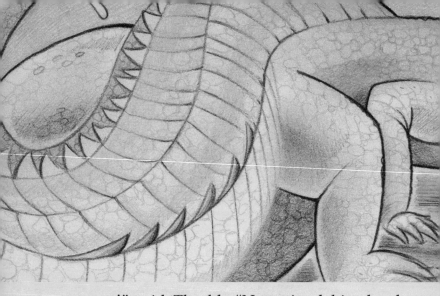

strong!" said Thudd. "No animal bite hard as super-crocodile bite. Not even Tyranno-saurus!"

Andrew left Thudd and the DNA Detector on a flat stone. He splashed into the water and yanked Judy up.

BROOOAAARRR!

A rumble like a terrible toilet flushing came from behind them. Andrew turned to see the crocodile lunge forward. It opened its mouth so wide, Uncle Al could have stood up inside it! It slammed its toothy jaws shut so fast that Andrew didn't see them close.

"Yeeeeeouch!" screamed Judy. "It's got my hair!"

The crocodile was pulling Judy backward through the water.

"*Yaaaaaaaaaaaaah!*" she screamed.

Andrew grabbed one of Judy's legs.

"Beeper!" yelled Andrew.

Beeper was holding Thudd up to his ear.

"Hoo boy!" yelled Beeper. "Thudd says we gotta hit the croc on the nose!"

He picked up a stone and threw it. It splashed down in front of Andrew.

Judy reached behind her. She began to

beat the crocodile on the nose with her fists.

Whap! Whap! Whap!

The crocodile snapped its jaws open for a second and Judy tugged her head away!

Beeper threw another rock. It landed in front of the crocodile. The crocodile dove to search for it.

Andrew and Judy scrambled out of the water. All three of them ran deeper into the forest.

After a few minutes, they were out of breath and stopped.

"Here ya go," said Beeper, handing Thudd back to Andrew.

meep . . . "Oody okey-dokey?" squeaked Thudd.

"Yeah," said Judy, "but my hair feels shorter."

Andrew broke off a large leaf from a tree and wrapped it around Thudd.

"My pockets are wet," he said, putting

Thudd in his pajama pocket. "This leaf will keep you dry."

RRROHHHURROHRR!

THUMMMPP . . . THUMMMPP . . . THUMMMPP . . .

The ground shook.

meep . . . "Tyrannosaurus come back!" squeaked Thudd.

"Not again!" hollered Judy.

Andrew couldn't see the dinosaur through the trees, but the thumps were getting louder.

KRAAAAAACK! KRUNNNCHHH!

Trees were snapping! The Tyrannosaurus was knocking them down!

They ran deeper into the forest. Andrew spied a rocky wall ahead. He couldn't see a way around it. They were trapped!

"We've got to climb that wall!" shouted Andrew.

Andrew started up first. The black rock

was jagged and rough on his bare feet, but he found places to step and places to grab. There were small trees growing between cracks in the rock. Andrew hung on to these, too, as he scrambled up.

"Hoo boy!" said Beeper, following. "This is better than the climbing wall at the mall. *They* make you wear a harness."

They reached a place where the rock wall was smooth and bare. Andrew couldn't see a way to get any farther up.

The Tyrannosaurus had reached the rock wall. Its scaly head was close to their feet.

RRROHHHURROHRR!

The sound shook Andrew's bones and made his ears ache.

The edge of Andrew's ledge began to crumble. He pushed his feet closer together.

Judy was standing on a ledge next to Andrew. Her ledge was crumbling, too.

"So what do we do now, Bug-Brain?" she

asked. "We're thirty seconds away from turning into a Tyranno-snack."

"Just hang on," said Andrew. "Maybe it will go away when it figures out it can't get us."

The Tyrannosaurus's tiny arms were ripping bushes out of the cliff. The dinosaur was trying to climb up! Pieces of stone cracked away from the cliff and rained down to the ground below.

"Or maybe it will wait till there's an avalanche and we fall into its mouth," said Judy.

Suddenly something thick and green dropped down in front of Andrew. It was a rope made of vines!

IT'S A BIRD! IT'S A PLANE! IT'S A FLYING LIZARD!

"It's safe," came a voice from above. "All three of you can climb up."

Andrew threw the end of the rope to Judy and she passed it to Beeper.

RRROHHHURROHRR!

Andrew climbed up quickly.

When he got close to the top of the cliff, he saw a tall woman in jeans and a T-shirt holding the rope. Long braids that hung all the way to her waist were tied back with a scarf.

"Well, hello, Andrew and Thudd!" she said, smiling. "And I see Judy right behind you."

"Hiya!" squeaked Thudd.

"Hi there!" said Andrew, hauling himself onto flat ground. "You must be Professor Wilde! But how do you know me and Judy?"

Winka laughed. "Your uncle Al talks about you *all* the time."

Judy and Beeper dragged themselves over the edge of the cliff.

Beeper went up to Winka and stuck out his hand. "I'm Beeper Jones," he said. "Doctor Kron-Tox is my uncle. I know he kidnapped you. He even parked *me* three hundred million years ago to collect bugs.

"My uncle is kinda weird. But I sure liked collecting the bugs, especially the dog-sized scorpion and the six-foot-long centipede."

Winka smiled and shook his hand. "Glad to meet you, Beeper. And I wish I had seen that centipede!

"But how did all of you end up here, sixty-five million years from your own time?"

"We came in the Time-A-Tron," said Judy. "We've got to find Uncle Al in some stupid ice age, and then we can all go back to our own time."

RRROHHHURROHRR!

"Oh, shut up!" said Judy, peering over the cliff at the Tyrannosaurus below.

Winka pushed her hands into the pockets of her jeans. "I don't know if you know this," said Winka. "But a terrible time is coming soon."

"Not *another* one!" said Judy, rolling her eyes. "We could write a big fat book about terrible times. We've gotten flushed down a toilet, swallowed by a whale, and trapped at the center of the Earth."

"This will be a disaster for the whole Earth," said Winka. "Very soon, an asteroid as big as a city will crash into the place where Mexico will be."

"That's nothing," said Andrew. "We were here when a Mars-sized asteroid crashed into the Earth and made the moon!"

Winka's eyebrows went up. "And you're alive to tell about it!" she said. "The asteroid that's coming won't rip the Earth apart, but it will make a terrible explosion. It will set huge fires, start mile-high tsunami waves, and send trillions of tons of dust and water into the air.

"The Earth will be covered by a dark cloud of dust for months. Plants will die. The big plant-eaters will die, and the big meat-eaters that eat the big plant-eaters will die.

"When it's over, animals that weigh more than fifty pounds will be gone."

"*I* weigh more than fifty pounds," said Judy. She looked around at the others. "We *all* do. We'd better get out of here *fast*."

"I'll go get my notebook," said Winka. "I've been drawing the animals and writing about them."

Winka turned to a tree behind her and started climbing. High above the ground, between the branches, she had woven a large net from vines.

Suddenly the sky darkened.

Andrew looked up. A huge creature was flying overhead.

meep . . . "Quetzalcoatlus!" said Thudd, pointing to his face screen.

"Yikes!" said Andrew. "That bird is as big as a plane!"

meep . . . "Not bird," said Thudd. "No birds on Earth yet. Flying animal is flying lizard."

"Quetzalcoatlus!" shouted Beeper. "That's my most favorite animal ever!"

"It's the biggest creature ever to fly," said

KETS-ahl-koh-AHT-lus

Winka, climbing down the tree. "It has a nest on the side of the cliff."

"I gotta see it!" yelled Beeper, taking off after the Quetzalcoatlus. "I gotta take a picture!"

"Beeper!" yelled Winka. "Come back here! We have to leave!"

Andrew and Judy ran through the trees after Beeper. Beyond the tall trees was a field. By the time Andrew and Judy reached the edge of the field, Beeper had disappeared among the tall ferns and bushes.

They watched the Quetzalcoatlus swoop low over the field.

Winka caught up with Andrew and Judy. "I'm worried about Beeper," she said. "That field is no place to be right now."

"Why not?" asked Andrew.

"You'll see," said Winka. "I'll lead the way to the Quetzalcoatlus nest. Stay right beside me."

Winka led them along the edge of the field. The ferns and palm-like plants were so tall that they couldn't see above them.

Now and then, Andrew saw wide paths through the field. It looked as though they had been flattened by a bulldozer.

"What happened there?" asked Andrew, pointing to the paths.

"Triceratops," said Winka. "That's what I'm worried about."

meep . . . "*Triceratops* mean 'three-horned face,'" said Thudd. "Triceratops got biggest head of any animal on land. One Triceratops weigh as much as three elephants."

"Weren't Triceratopses kind of like giant cows?" asked Judy. "All they did was eat plants."

"That's true," said Winka. "They're usually peaceful plant-eaters. But—"

There was a rustling sound close by, then a stomping sound. The ground shook.

"It's Triceratops mating season," said Winka. "Get into the trees. Hurry!"

try-SEHR-uh-tops

9 OPEN WIDE!

From the forest, they could see a clearing. Two Triceratopses were charging toward each other.

The huge animals looked like enormous rhinoceroses. But these creatures were as long as classrooms, tall as ceilings, and wide as buses!

They had beaks like parrots and short horns behind their beaks. Above their eyes were horns as long as a man's leg. Bony collars stood up behind their heads.

KRAAAAACK!

Their heads butted hard. The horns above

their eyes locked together. Each Triceratops was trying to drag the other one to the ground.

"The males fight and the winners get a mate," said Winka in a low voice. "After a while, there'll be eggs that hatch into baby Triceratopses.

"We'd better catch up with Beeper. He's probably gotten to the Quetzalcoatlus's nest by now."

Judy rolled her eyes. "If Bozo-Boy hasn't gotten himself trampled by a Triceratops," she said.

They trekked to the edge of a cliff bordered by craggy rocks.

Between the rocks, Andrew spied the soles of a pair of sneakers.

Beeper had hooked his feet between the rocks and was hanging upside down over the cliff!

"Beeper!" yelled Andrew. He dove down

and grabbed Beeper's right ankle.

"Hoo boy!" came Beeper's voice from below. "Look at that! Four babies in the nest. There's an egg, too!"

"Beeper," said Winka sternly. "Those rocks could come loose. We'll pull you back up."

She grabbed Beeper's left foot.

"Just a minute," he said. "I'm taking a picture. Aw! Look at that one! It's flapping its wings!"

Scrummmmp

Suddenly the edge of the cliff started to crumble. Beeper was slipping down! His left shoe came off in Winka's hands, but Andrew still had hold of Beeper's ankle.

Then Andrew was sliding, too!

"Yowzers!" he cried as he flipped over the cliff.

Still gripping Beeper's ankle, Andrew swung through the air. He found himself

hanging from Beeper's ankle over the Quet-zalcoatlus's nest!

"My T-shirt got caught on a branch!" yelled Beeper. "Uh-oh! My shirt is ripping. We're gonna fall!"

"Andrew!" yelled Winka. "Let go of Beeper. If you both crash into the nest, it might break and you could fall a long way. But the nest should be strong enough for just you."

Andrew took a deep breath and let go.

Gack! cackled the little Quetzalcoatluses as Andrew landed between them. *Gack! Gack!*

The babies were the size of thin turkeys. Their bodies were covered with soft fuzz and their wings were covered with skin as thin as paper. Their long beaks were open. They looked hungry.

"Good work, Andrew!" said Winka. "Judy is gathering some vines to use as a rope. Beeper's shirt could rip any second, so we'll get him first."

Winka lowered the vines to Beeper. Judy helped to pull him up.

"Now it's your turn, Andrew," said Winka.

A shadow came over the nest. The mother Quetzalcoatlus was circling overhead!

"Bit of a problem, Andrew," said Winka. "The mother is coming to feed the chicks. She could get quite nasty if she thinks we're bothering her nest. I'm afraid you'll have to stay there until she's finished."

"Um, what am I supposed to do while she's feeding the babies?" asked Andrew.

"Well," said Winka. "The only safe thing to do is to act just like a chick. She might toss you out of the nest if she thinks you don't belong to her."

The airplane-sized lizard glided close to the nest with her wings spread wide.

Thump!

The nest shook as she landed on the edge. A breeze ruffled Andrew's hair as the Quetzalcoatlus fluttered her enormous wings and folded them next to her body.

Uh-oh, thought Andrew. *What's that brown gunky stuff in her beak?*

The chicks crowded around their mother and opened their beaks wider. She crammed some of the lumpy brown gunk into each waiting beak.

Then the Quetzalcoatlus shoved her long beak toward Andrew's mouth.

10 NOMORESAURUSES

"Yerghhh!" groaned Andrew, jerking his head away. "It smells like dead fish!"

meep . . . "Gotta open mouth," said Thudd softly. "And gotta not talk. Gotta act like Quetzalcoatlus chick."

"Do I have to?" whispered Andrew.

"Yoop," whispered Thudd.

"Um . . . *Gack!*" squawked Andrew. "*Gack! Gack!*"

He flapped his arms, closed his eyes, and opened his mouth.

Something lumpy dropped onto his tongue. It was sandy, salty, and squishy.

Andrew opened his eyes. The mother Quetzalcoatlus was using her beak to pick through the fuzz on her body.

meep . . . "Scales of reptiles turn into fur for Quetzalcoatlus and feathers for birds," said Thudd. "Feather is just different kind of scale."

Andrew spat the squishy stuff out of his mouth. A baby Quetzalcoatlus dove to eat it up.

The mother Quetzalcoatlus spread her wings, leaned forward, and launched herself into the air.

"Holy moly!" yelled Andrew. "Get me out of here!"

"You did a great job, Andrew!" said Winka, lowering the vines down to the nest. "Wrap this around your waist and we'll bring you up."

Andrew twisted the vines around his middle and hung on with both hands as Winka, Judy, and Beeper pulled.

"Thanks!" he said as he tugged himself over the edge.

"Well," sighed Winka. "We'd better get back to the Time-A-Tron before one of you gets yourself adopted—or eaten—by some giant reptile."

Just then, the big purple button in the middle of Thudd's chest popped open. A beam of purple light zoomed out. But Uncle Al wasn't at the end of it.

"Oh no!" said Judy. "It's Doctor Kron-Tox again!"

tick . . . tock . . . tick . . . tock . . .

"Hello, Dubbles,
And Winka, too.
You can't see me,
But I see you.

Do you know
The Earth's in trouble?
And so are *you*,
My little Dubbles!

The rock that ends
The dinos' day
Is coming now,
It's on its way.

How sad you're stuck
In such a fix.
You're at the end
Of all your tricks.

But please don't fret,
My little pups.
I'll soon be there
To scoop you up!

HA HA HA HA HA!"
tick . . . tock . . . tick . . . tock . . .
Winka scanned the sky. "I don't see any-thing yet," she said. "But Doctor Kron-Tox has telescopes. We'd better get going. Where's the Time-A-Tron?"

"It's beyond a big pond of quicksand," said Judy. "Next to a Tyrannosaurus nest."

"Ah!" said Winka. "I know the place, and I know a shortcut. Let's go."

Winka led them downhill to a place where the cliff wasn't far from the valley below. Winka used the vine rope to lower them down, then she climbed down herself.

"There's something we have to do before we go back," said Andrew.

"We must leave as soon as possible," said Winka. "We're far from where the asteroid will crash, but the explosion will start huge forest fires even here. Tsunami waves could flood this place."

Andrew nodded. "I know," he said, "but an owl escaped from the Time-A-Tron when we landed. We're not supposed to leave anything here."

Beeper pulled the DNA Detector out of his pocket.

Winka cocked her head. "Professor Dubble and I invented the DNA Detector together," she said. "It's quite handy."

Andrew punched in "northern pygmy owl" and pressed the Find It button.

ping . . . ping . . . ping . . .

"3,000 Feet" blinked the display.

They trudged through the ferns and bushes. They crossed over Tyrannosaurus tracks.

"2,000 Feet" blinked the display.

The landscape started to look familiar.

"1,000 Feet" blinked the display.

"I see one of the Time-A-Tron's fins!" said Winka. She was tall enough to see above the ferns.

"The DNA Detector says the owl is only three hundred feet away!" said Andrew.

They ran to the Time-A-Tron. It was still leaning against the Tyrannosaurus nest.

"Look!" said Judy, pointing to an egg that hadn't yet hatched. On top of the egg was the owl! Its eyes were closed.

"It's trying to hatch a Tyrannosaurus!" said Beeper.

"It's asleep," said Winka.

Winka untied the scarf that held back her braids. She tiptoed behind the nest, stretched the scarf above the owl, and pulled it down fast.

Hoooo hoooo hoooo

"Sorry to wake you," said Winka. She wrapped the owl up in her scarf and held it firmly. Then she covered the Tyrannosaurus egg with moss and leaves to protect it.

bong . . . The door of the Time-A-Tron opened.

They all piled into the bottom compartment.

bong . . . The door closed.

Winka placed the owl on top of the tachyon fuel tank and opened the scarf.

bong . . . "Children!" said the Time-A-Tron. "You are safe, and you've brought Professor Wilde! And, Professor Wilde, you've captured the owl! You are all heroes!"

"We have to leave right away," said Andrew, scrambling up to the top compartment.

"There's another stupid asteroid coming," said Judy, following Andrew.

"It's gonna wipe out the dinosaurs," said Beeper quietly. He kicked a pile of tachyon tubes.

"And Doctor Kron-Tox is on his way,"

said Winka. "Come on, Beeper. We've got work to do."

meep . . . "Look!" said Thudd, pointing to a bright dot moving slowly across the sky. The dot grew larger and larger, like a balloon filling with air.

"That's it," said Winka. "We don't have long."

meep . . . "Asteroid travel one hundred twenty-five miles every second!" said Thudd.

bong . . .

Behind Andrew and Judy's seat, another chair was rising from the floor.

bong . . . "For you, Professor Wilde," said the Time-A-Tron.

They all buckled themselves quickly into their seats.

BAROOOOOOOOOOM!

The Earth shook and rose like a giant wave on the ocean.

meep . . . "Asteroid crash make giant

earthquake!" said Thudd.

The sky exploded into rivers of blinding yellow-white fire.

"I can't see the control panel!" yelled Judy. "I can't find the Fast-Forward button."

"Look for the button with your fingers, Judy," said Winka.

bong . . . "But whatever you do," said the Time-A-Tron, "do NOT press the Fast-Back button! We do not have a drop of fuel to waste traveling to the past!"

"I think I've got the right button," said Judy, pounding it.

Flack! Flack! Flack!

HNNNNN . . . HNNNNN . . . HNNNNN . . .

Only one of the Fast-Fins began spinning. The Time-A-Tron was lying on its side and the other Fast-Fin was stuck in the dirt.

WOOHOOOOOO!

The one moving Fast-Fin sent balls of green fire swirling around the Time-A-Tron.

65 MILLION YEARS AGO blinked the display on the control panel. But the numbers weren't changing.

Uh-oh, thought Andrew. *I sure hope we don't end up as Dubble fossils!*

TO BE CONTINUED IN ANDREW, JUDY, AND THUDD'S
NEXT EXCITING ADVENTURE:

ANDREW LOST
IN THE ICE AGE!

In stores October 2005

THUDD

TRUE STUFF

Thudd wanted to tell you more about the Earth as it was 65 million years ago, but he was too busy keeping his friends from being eaten by Tyrannosauruses and Quetzalcoatluses. Here's what he wanted to say:

• Brains come in different shapes and sizes. We can tell a lot about an animal by examining its brain.

For example, smell is very important to dogs, and the parts of a dog's brain that receive smell messages—the olfactory lobes—are very large. Four times as large as the olfactory lobes of humans! From this, we can tell that dogs depend much more on their sense of smell than humans do.

The skulls of Tyrannosauruses show us that they, too, had big olfactory lobes. They must have been great sniffers!

• We're not absolutely sure what Tyrannosauruses used their great noses for. Some people believe they were hunters. Others believe they were scavengers, that they sniffed out—and ate—dead animals. Maybe they did both!

• Not long ago, a three-year-old boy named David Shiffler found a "pebble" while on a camping trip with his parents. He insisted it was a dinosaur egg.

His parents didn't believe a three-year-old could know anything about dinosaur eggs, but they did take the little stone to a paleontologist, someone who studies fossils.

It turned out that the pebble was—yes!— a dinosaur egg. It was also the oldest meat-eating dinosaur egg ever found!

Who knows what *you* could find someday?

• In the name "Bambiraptor," the "bambi" part comes from the Italian word *bambino*, which means "baby." This name was given to the Bambiraptor dinosaur because it was so small—only three feet long and one foot tall. At first, scientists thought it was a baby and not a full-grown dinosaur!

The first Bambiraptor fossil was found by a fourteen-year-old boy named Wes Linster.

• Quicksand is just regular sand mixed with lots of water that comes up from underneath it.

• No one knows for sure what sounds dinosaurs made. But by studying the shapes of their heads and throats and comparing them to living animals, scientists can make guesses about what dinosaurs may have sounded like.

• The biggest plant-eating dinosaurs were *much* bigger than the biggest meat-eaters.

For example, the giant plant-eating Argentinosaurus (it was found in the South American country of Argentina) was longer than three school buses and weighed more than twenty elephants!

The Tyrannosaurus rex was only about as long as one school bus and it weighed less than one big elephant!

• There are colorful words to describe groups of animals: a gaggle of geese, a pride of lions, a leap of leopards, a parliament of owls. Can you think of names for groups of dinosaurs? A terror of Tyrannosauruses?

• Alligators have little black dots all over their faces. Not long ago, a scientist named Daphne Soares figured out that these dots are sensors. They allow the alligator to feel even the smallest movement in the water. Crocodiles have similar sensors all over their bodies!

• Many things can become fossils, even dino poop! Fossilized poop is called a coprolite. The "-lite" part of this word means "rock."

• Some scientists think that when the giant asteroid smashed into the Earth 65 million years ago, it threw up a wall of dirt and rock that reached halfway to the moon!

WHERE TO FIND MORE TRUE STUFF

Want to find out more about some of the weirdest creatures that have ever lived on Earth? Read these books!

• *Dinosaurs! The Biggest Baddest Strangest Fastest* by Howard Zimmerman (New York: Atheneum, 2000). Would you like to meet a thirty-foot-long Therizinosaurus with two-foot-long claws? You can do it safely in this book.

• *Beyond the Dinosaurs! Sky Dragons Sea Monsters Mega-Mammals and Other Prehistoric Beasts* by Howard Zimmerman (New York: Atheneum, 2001). Not every bizarre creature that lived millions of years ago was a dino-saur. Get to know other ones here!

• *Extreme Dinosaurs* by Luis V. Rey (San

Francisco: Chronicle Books, 2001). This book has fantastic paintings of dino action in the landscapes you would have seen millions of years ago.

• *T. Rex: Hunter or Scavenger?* by Dr. Thomas R. Holtz, Jr. (New York: Random House, 2003).

• *Raptor Pack* by Dr. Robert T. Bakker (New York: Random House, 2003). Hang out with raptors for a day!

• *Maximum Triceratops* by Dr. Robert T. Bakker (New York: Random House, 2004). Spend time with a feisty vegetarian!

Turn the page
for a sneak peek at
Andrew, Judy, and Thudd's
next exciting adventure—

ANDREW LOST
IN THE ICE AGE

Available October 2005

ARE WE THERE YET?

Why are we stuck in dinosaur time? thought ten-year-old Andrew Dubble, strapped inside the Time-A-Tron time-travel vehicle. Outside, a forest fire was roaring closer. *Why aren't we heading for the ice age?*

Sitting next to Andrew, his thirteen-year-old cousin Judy was furiously pounding a button on the control panel.

"This better be the Fast-Forward button!" she said.

An asteroid the size of a city had just slammed into the Earth and set off an enormous explosion. It had heated the surface of the Earth to a thousand degrees and started fires all around the world.

"Oops!" came a voice from the backseat. It was Beeper Jones, the boy they had rescued 300 million years ago. "I lost my camera. I think it fell off my belt when I was getting into the Time-A-Tron. I gotta go get it. It's got the only pictures of dinos ever taken!"

"Oh no you don't," said Professor Winka Wilde, grabbing him by the neck of his T-shirt.

"The fire will be here in seconds and the air may be too hot to breathe," said Winka.

Beeper yanked himself away. In an instant he had pulled up the door in the floor and jumped down into the lower compartment.

"Beeper!" yelled Winka Wilde. "Get back here!"